AI

Ronald and Candace: A Love Story

Copyright © 2024 by AI

All rights reserved. No part of this publication may be reproduced, stored or transmitted in any form or by any means, electronic, mechanical, photocopying, recording, scanning, or otherwise without written permission from the publisher. It is illegal to copy this book, post it to a website, or distribute it by any other means without permission.

First edition

This book was professionally typeset on Reedsy. Find out more at reedsy.com

Contents

I   The Pact

1	Graduation Day	3
2	The News	6
3	Meeting Nancy	10
4	The Wedding	14

II   Court of Fangs and Claws

5	The Arrangement	21
6	Vows of the Night	25
7	Court	29
8	The Dungeon	33

III   Ronald + Candace

9	Part I: The Meeting	41
10	Part II: The Balcony	43
11	Part III: Banishment	45
12	Part IV: A Tragic Reunion	47

IV   Breaking the Ice

13	Worlds Collide	53
14	Lessons in Literature	57

| 15 | Thin Ice | 61 |
| 16 | The Big Game | 65 |

V Power and Passion

17	The Snare	71
18	Cracks in the Mask	74
19	Alliances and Affection	78
20	The Sickle and The Eagle	82

VI Love Across The Eras

21	A Brush With Time	89
22	Out of Place	92
23	A Night To Remember	95
24	I Will Find You	98

I

The Pact

A Friends to Lovers Romance

1

Graduation Day

The sun hung low in the sky, casting a warm orange glow over the campus as the final day of college life for Ronald Reagan and Candace Sharp arrived. It was graduation day, and the air buzzed with excitement, anticipation, and the bittersweet realization that life as they knew it was about to change.

Ronald adjusted his cap, smoothing out the creases of his robe. His eyes wandered over the sea of students, all caught up in the whirlwind of emotions that came with this momentous day. But his gaze kept returning to one person: Candace. She stood a few feet away, scanning the crowd, her brown curls caught in the breeze. Her green eyes, always bright with curiosity and laughter, reflected the same emotions he felt.

"Well, here we are," he said, walking up to her. His voice cracked slightly, betraying the nerves he was trying to hide. "The end of the line."

Candace smiled, her lips curving upward with a hint of sadness. "I know," she said, her voice soft but steady. "It doesn't feel real. Like we've been living in some kind of dream for the past four years. And now… we're waking up."

They both fell silent, taking in the familiar sights—the quad where they spent hours talking, the dorms they'd snuck into for late-night chats, the café where they'd shared countless cups of coffee. Their friendship had been forged in the fires of mischief, late-night study sessions, and endless laughter. College had been their playground, a world where the rules of adulthood didn't quite apply yet. They had had so much fun, too much to count, and yet here they were, at the precipice of adulthood, about to embark on different paths.

"I'm going to miss this," Candace said, finally breaking the silence. "I'm going to miss you, Ronald."

Ronald swallowed, his throat suddenly dry. "I know. I'll miss you too. It's… it's weird, you know? We've spent so much time together, and now we're… we're just supposed to walk away from it all?"

Candace turned to face him fully, her expression serious. "We're not walking away. We're just… going in different directions. But that doesn't mean we're leaving each other behind."

Ronald nodded, but the lump in his throat grew larger. He had never been good with goodbyes, and this one felt harder than any of the others. He looked at Candace, his best friend—the person who had been there through every awkward phase, every triumph, every failure.

"You know, I've been thinking," he said, his voice a little unsteady, "about how crazy it is that we're both heading off to different cities. Different lives. I mean, you're going to chase your dream job, and I… I don't even know what I'm doing yet. Actor? Politician? Who knows! But it feels like we've been through everything together. And now we're just… splitting apart."

Candace reached out and placed a hand on his shoulder. "We're not splitting apart. We'll always be friends. No matter where life takes us, we'll always have each other. And when things get tough, you know I'll be there."

He looked at her, feeling the weight of her words. "Yeah. I know you will."

They stood there for a moment, just taking it all in, the realization settling in that their college years were over. The next chapter of their lives was just around the corner, but the thought of stepping into it without each other felt impossible.

Candace's eyes sparkled with a sudden thought. "You know what we should do?" she asked, her voice mischievous.

"What?"

"We should make a pact. A ridiculous, crazy pact."

Ronald raised an eyebrow. "A pact? What kind of pact?"

"A pact that, if neither of us is married by the time we're 40, we'll marry each other."

Ronald's face lit up with surprise. "Wait, what? You're serious?"

Candace shrugged, a playful grin tugging at her lips. "Why not? We've been best friends for four years. We've had more fun than most people can imagine. And who knows? Maybe, just maybe, we'll both end up single when we hit 40. We might as well have something to look forward to."

Ronald stared at her for a moment, his heart pounding in his chest. He couldn't help but laugh. "You're out of your mind. But… okay. Let's do it. If neither of us is married by 40, we'll get married. It's a deal."

"Deal." Candace extended her hand, and Ronald shook it firmly, sealing their pact.

For a moment, they stood there, both of them caught in the gravity of the decision they'd just made. But despite the silliness of it all, it felt strangely comforting. No matter where life took them, they would always have this promise to fall back on.

And as the final bells of graduation rang out, signaling the end of one chapter and the beginning of another, Ronald Reagan and Candace Sharp knew that, no matter what the future held, they would always have each other.

2

The News

Candace Sharp's mornings were always a whirlwind. She woke up before the sun, ran a few miles to clear her head, and was in the office by 7 a.m. ready to conquer the world. New York City was her empire, and she was its queen. She had built her career from the ground up, slowly carving her path in the competitive world of finance. Her reputation as a boss babe—a woman who was equal parts brilliant and relentless—was cemented, and there was no room for distractions.

At 32, Candace had mastered the art of keeping people at arm's length. She didn't have time for relationships. Men came and went, but nothing ever lasted. She was a force to be reckoned with, too focused, too independent to let anyone get too close. Her friends, when she had time for them, understood that she couldn't afford to care about anything that wasn't her career. She'd been burned too many times by fleeting romances to trust anyone with her heart.

But as she sat in her sleek Manhattan apartment, sipping her second cup of coffee, something on her phone caught her eye. She scrolled absently through her news feed until one headline stopped her dead in her tracks:

"Hollywood Heartthrob Ronald Reagan Engaged to Longtime Girlfriend Nancy."

The words blurred before her eyes as she stared at the screen, the coffee mug trembling slightly in her hand. Her stomach did a strange flip, a sensation she hadn't felt in years. She blinked hard and read the headline again as if it might change. But it didn't. Ronald Reagan, her best friend from college, the boy who had made her laugh until her stomach hurt, the boy who had been her rock through every late-night conversation, was engaged to someone else.

Nancy. She had always known that the moment Ronald stepped into the spotlight, he would find a beauty who could match his new life. And why not? He was a movie star now, with a career that had soared to heights Candace could never have imagined.

But still… it hurt. A small, almost imperceptible ache in her chest, one that she quickly suppressed. They had made a pact, hadn't they? They'd promised that if they were both single at 40, they'd marry each other. But that was just a silly, youthful promise, made in the heat of graduation day. It was never supposed to be real. She was fine. She was fine.

But she wasn't fine.

The ache refused to go away, gnawing at her as she threw herself into her work. She arrived at her office late and in a daze, forcing herself to focus on the tasks at hand. But the news of Ronald's engagement clung to her like a thick fog, clouding her every thought.

At 10 a.m., during a crucial meeting, Candace's mind wandered. She fumbled through her presentation, glossing over key points, and her audience quickly lost interest. In a slip of concentration, she mistakenly referred to her client as "Ronald" and called his assistant "Nancy," even though their names were Martin and Kate. The silence in the room felt suffocating as she realized her mistake, but no matter how hard she tried, she couldn't snap out of the fog clouding her thoughts. She could feel the weight of her colleagues' disappointed stares, but it was as if she were watching everything unfold from a distance, unable to regain control.

When the meeting finally ended, she retreated to her office, closing the door behind her with a soft click. She slumped into her chair, running her fingers through her hair, frustrated with herself. This wasn't like her. She was always in control, always the one who had everything together. But today, it felt like her world was slowly unraveling.

Lunch passed in a blur, and by 2 p.m., she was spilling her Trader Joe's gingerbread-flavored coffee all over her desk. She cursed under her breath as she scrambled to clean up the mess. She had never been so clumsy in her life. It felt like the universe was conspiring against her, reminding her that she wasn't as untouchable as she liked to think.

By the time the workday was winding down, Candace found herself staring blankly at her computer screen, watching cat videos. The office was nearly empty, the hum of fluorescent lights the only sound in the room. She should have been heading home, but she couldn't bring herself to leave. She was too distracted, too lost in the thoughts of Ronald and Nancy.

And then, as if on cue, her phone rang. The name on the screen made her stomach flip again.

Ronald Reagan.

Her heart skipped a beat as she hesitated, then quickly swiped the screen to answer. She hadn't spoken to him in months—busy lives, busy schedules—but she couldn't ignore him. She had to answer.

"Hey, Ronald," she said, trying to sound casual, but her voice wavered slightly.

"Candace," he said, his voice warm and familiar, and for a moment, everything felt normal again. "How's my favorite boss babe?"

"Same old, same old. You know how it is. Busy, crazy… You?"

"I'm good, really good," he replied. There was a brief pause, and Candace could almost hear the smile in his voice. "So, I've got a question for you."

"Okay… shoot."

"I'm getting married in a few months, you probably saw it in the news, considering I'm everywhere," he said, and Candace's breath caught in her throat. She had known it was coming, but hearing him say it out loud still made her heart ache. "And I wanted to ask if you could come. You're one of my closest friends, Candace. I can't imagine not having you there."

Candace felt a lump form in her throat. She was happy for him, truly, but hearing his voice, knowing that he was about to embark on this huge milestone without her by his side in the way she had once imagined—it stung.

But she forced a smile. "Of course, I'll be there. Wouldn't miss it for the world."

"Great," Ronald said, his voice genuine. "I'll send you the details, and we'll figure out the rest later. I can't wait to see you, Candace."

"I can't wait either," she replied, her voice quieter than she'd intended. She could hear the line click, and the call ended with a soft beep.

She sat there for a long time, her phone still pressed to her ear as she stared at the screen. She had said the right thing, of course. She'd be there for Ronald, just like she always had been. But as the seconds ticked by, she couldn't shake the feeling that everything had changed.

3

Meeting Nancy

Candace stepped off the plane and into the warm Los Angeles air, her heels clicking on the terminal floor as she made her way through the crowd. She hadn't been to California in years, and as she caught a glimpse of the palm trees swaying in the distance, something about the city felt both familiar and foreign. It wasn't like New York, that's for sure. But today, the sunshine felt like a welcome change from the gray clouds that had settled over her mind ever since she'd gotten the call.

Ronald was waiting for her at the gate. She spotted him right away, tall and effortlessly handsome, his face lighting up when he saw her. It was like no time had passed at all. He still had that easy grin that could make anyone feel at ease. And just like in college, he was dressed casually—dark jeans and a navy T-shirt that clung just right to his shoulders.

"Candace!" he exclaimed, pulling her into a hug. "You look amazing."

She chuckled, hugging him back. "I haven't seen you in forever, Ronald. You look like you haven't aged a day."

"Hollywood magic," he said with a wink, stepping back to take a good look at her.

"I'm glad you could make it. Nancy's been dying to meet you," He motioned behind him. Candace followed his gaze to see a woman standing just a few feet away. She had a bright, welcoming smile, but Candace could tell she was trying to be polite without being overly excited. She had that polished, perfect look—someone who fit the image of Ronald Reagan's fiance.

"Nancy, this is Candace," Ronald introduced, and Candace took a step forward to offer her hand.

"It's so great to finally meet you!" Nancy said, shaking Candace's hand firmly. "Ronald's told me so much about you."

Candace smiled, trying to mask the odd sensation stirring in her chest. "It's great to meet you too. Ronald's told me a lot about you as well."

"Only good things, I hope," Nancy said with a laugh, a little nervousness in her voice.

Candace merely shrugged in response. Her friendship with Ronald suddenly felt a little more complicated than she'd ever anticipated.

They piled into a car, and as the drive to a local restaurant unfolded, Candace couldn't help but notice the way Ronald and Nancy interacted. They were comfortable with each other, of course, but there was an intimacy there that Candace hadn't expected. The way Nancy would laugh at Ronald's jokes before he even finished, or the soft hand she placed on his arm when they stopped at a red light. It was all so… domestic. So real. And it made Candace feel like an outsider.

When they arrived at the restaurant, a chic spot in downtown LA with floor-to-ceiling windows and a view of the city's sprawling skyline, Candace felt like a small-town girl in a glittering world. She had never been the type to worry about appearances, but now, as they were led to a private table, the weight of it all hit her.

Nancy, in contrast, seemed right at home. She slid into the seat next to Ronald, engaging him in quiet conversation as the menus were handed out. Candace sat across from them, trying to force a smile while her mind whirled.

The conversation started off light—small talk about LA, about the weather, about Candace's work life. But soon, Ronald and Candace began to drift into their own world.

"Remember that time we snuck into the library to study, and then spent hours laughing instead of studying?" Ronald said with a grin, his eyes twinkling as he turned toward Candace.

Candace laughed, shaking her head. "How could I forget? We ended up getting kicked out!And you tried to convince the librarian that we were 'conducting research on the psychological effects of laughter.'"

Ronald laughed loudly, leaning back in his chair. "It was a solid argument. But, yeah, I don't think she bought it."

Nancy gave a polite smile but didn't quite seem to know how to join in. She tried, though. "That sounds like a lot of fun. I was never much of a rebel in college. I just… focused on my studies."

Ronald didn't seem to hear Nancy, his eyes fixed on Candace. "Yeah, those were the best days. The late-night talks, the ridiculous pranks, the memories… Do you remember the possessed girl with the ghost boyfriend who died in the war?"

Candace burst into giggles. "How could I forget! That was when I moved into your apartment to escape her!"

Nancy's smile faltered for just a moment, but she quickly recovered, sipping her water. "It must have been nice to have that kind of bond. I guess it's good to have someone you can count on like that."

Candace blinked, suddenly remembering Nancy. She could feel the subtle tension now like the air was thickening between them. Nancy was trying so hard to relate, but her effort was too obvious. It wasn't that Candace disliked her—it was just… hard. Hard to sit across from the woman who now had the place in Ronald's life that Candace once held.

The meal continued, but Candace felt like a ghost in the room. Ronald, oblivious to the tension, kept steering the conversation back to their college days. He kept glancing at her, his eyes lingering just a little too long. Candace tried to smile, tried to participate, but the knot in her stomach only tightened as Ronald leaned toward her, his affection unmistakable.

Nancy cleared her throat, making an attempt to salvage the conversation, "So, how are things at work, Candace? You never really told me what you do."

Candace opened her mouth to respond, but before she could, Ronald's hand found Nancy's, giving it a soft squeeze. "Candace's company is huge now. She's crushing it," he said, his tone soft but with an underlying pride.

Nancy smiled, though it didn't quite reach her eyes. She shifted uncomfortably, and Candace could tell she was trying to hold it together, but the cracks were starting to show. Both women stared at each other for a long moment.

As the meal ended and they left the restaurant, Candace tried to shake the unease from her shoulders. She wasn't a jealous person—she'd never been. But now, with Ronald so clearly in love and Nancy holding his attention in a way that Candace couldn't, it all felt like a strange version of the friendship they'd once shared.

Ronald dropped her off at her hotel soon after, and Candace stood in the lobby, watching his car disappear down the street with a heaviness in her chest. The reality of everything hit her hard, and for the first time in years, she felt completely out of place.

* * *

Back at his house, Ronald and Nancy walked inside, hand in hand. Nancy immediately launched into talk about the wedding plans—flowers, seating arrangements, dress fittings—while Ronald nodded absently, his mind elsewhere. He wasn't listening to her. His thoughts kept drifting back to Candace. He hadn't realized just how much he missed her until he'd seen her again. The years had passed, but some things hadn't changed.

He missed the way Candace had always known how to make him laugh. He missed the way she understood him without words. And, despite everything, he couldn't help but think about the pact they'd made so long ago. The one where, if they were still single at 40, they would marry each other.

Ronald didn't say it aloud, but the thought lingered in the back of his mind as Nancy prattled on. He tried to focus on her, but all he could think about was Candace.

4

The Wedding

The church was beautiful—elegant, serene, and utterly fitting for a Hollywood wedding. Candles flickered softly in the dim light, casting shadows on the walls as a string quartet played a gentle melody. The air was thick with anticipation, as everyone took their seats, turning to watch the ceremony unfold.

Ronald Reagan stood at the altar, his back straight, hands trembling at his sides. He was supposed to be a movie star, a man who had everything figured out, but at this moment, he felt small. The wedding was everything his publicist had told him it should be—perfect, polished, and full of pageantry. But in the pit of his stomach, something was wrong. Something was missing.

He glanced down the aisle, his heart racing in his chest, but it wasn't Nancy he was looking at. His gaze drifted to the back of the church, where Candace sat, trying—unsuccessfully—to blend into the shadows. He could see her clearly, even from across the room. Her dark hair fell in waves around her shoulders, and her eyes, wide and apprehensive, were trained on the floor. She was sitting by herself, far from the others, her dress a simple black number that made him feel a little heated.

The music began. The sound of the bridal march filled the space, and everyone stood. Ronald's heart pounded, his hands growing clammy as he tried to focus on the woman walking toward him. Nancy looked stunning in her white gown, her smile radiant, but it wasn't her that Ronald saw. His eyes locked with Candace's again, and for a moment, he forgot everything. The ceremony, the expectations, the world. It was just him and Candace—just like it had always been.

For the briefest moment, he felt something like regret twist inside of him. *What am I doing?*

He tried to refocus on Nancy as she walked down the aisle, but the words of the preacher blurred, and the images of flowers, vows, and promises faded. All that was real, all that mattered, was Candace. He had promised her once—promised himself once—that if they were still single at 40, they would marry each other. And here he was, standing in front of a woman he barely knew in his heart, while the woman who had been by his side for years—who had made him laugh, who had been there for him when no one else had—sat quietly in the back, as though she was no longer a part of his story.

When Nancy arrived at the altar, she smiled up at him, her hands gently resting in his. The preacher began the ceremony, but Ronald barely heard the words. He felt trapped. His heart was somewhere else, somewhere he couldn't ignore any longer.

"I'm sorry," he blurted out, cutting off the preacher mid-sentence. He turned to Nancy, his face flushed with confusion and an unexpected sense of clarity. "I can't do this."

Nancy's smile faltered, and a ripple of confusion passed through the guests. "What?" she whispered, her voice shaking slightly.

"I'm sorry, Nancy," Ronald said again, his voice more certain now, though still edged with guilt. "I thought this was what I wanted. I thought you were who I needed. But I was wrong."

He turned away from her abruptly, his gaze fixed on Candace in the back of the church. He could feel the weight of everyone's eyes on him, but in that moment, nothing mattered except what he had to do next.

He walked quickly toward the back of the church, his footsteps echoing in the silence. As he reached Candace, she stood up, her face pale, her eyes wide with shock. Without thinking, he grabbed her hand—firm, urgent—and began pulling her toward the altar.

The gasps from the guests filled the air, but Ronald didn't care. His heart was pounding, his mind racing, and all he could focus on was Candace. He needed her. He had always needed her.

"Wait, what are you doing?" Nancy's voice came from behind him, her words thick with confusion and hurt.

Ronald didn't answer. He didn't need to. He led Candace up the aisle, all eyes on them now, a mixture of whispers and disbelief filling the church. He could feel the heat of their stares, but it didn't matter. Candace was with him, and that was all that mattered.

When they reached the altar, he turned to face the preacher, who stood frozen, unsure of what was happening.

"I'm sorry," Ronald said again, his voice loud and clear. "But it needs to be her. It's always been her."

Candace looked at him in shock, her hand still in his, her fingers trembling. She looked out at the crowd, then back at him, but Ronald could see the recognition in her eyes. She understood. She didn't need to ask questions, because she had always known. They had both known, deep down.

The preacher, after a long pause, seemed to accept what was happening. He cleared his throat and asked, "Do you—"

"Yes," Ronald interrupted, his voice stronger now. "Yes, I do. I want Candace."

The crowd sat in stunned silence, but then Nancy ran off, her tears trailing down her face as she fled from the church. Her departure only deepened the stillness in the room.

And then there was just Ronald and Candace. She stood there, looking at him, her face unreadable, but her eyes softening as she began to process what was happening. Slowly, she nodded.

"I'll marry you, Ronald," she said, her voice barely a whisper but filled with certainty. "I'll marry you."

The preacher, who had been holding his breath, nodded, motioning for them to join hands. The wedding that had been meant for another was now theirs. The vows were spoken, and everything felt right. It felt real.

As the ceremony ended and the crowd began to stand, Ronald's heart swelled with something he couldn't quite name. He turned to Candace, his eyes shining with a mix of joy and relief.

"I can rule the world with you by my side," he said, his voice full of conviction.

Candace smiled softly, her eyes brimming with tears. For the first time in years, she felt like everything had finally fallen into place. And in that moment, with everyone watching them, they knew their journey had only just begun.

II

Court of Fangs and Claws

A Fantasy Enemies To Lovers Romance

5

The Arrangement

The grand dining hall of the estate was bathed in the soft glow of chandelier light, casting long shadows over the opulent table. Candace Sharp, Princess of the Vampires, sat at one end of a long table, her pale, perfect features framed by flowing brown hair. Her ruby-red gown shimmered like a second skin, clinging to her slender frame as she surveyed the room with an air of detached superiority. She hated this. The forced diplomacy. The grotesque pretenses.

Across from her, Ronald Reagan, the Prince of the Werewolves, exuded an aura of raw power and celebrity. A ruggedly handsome man with striking amber eyes and tousled dark hair, he was the very picture of the type of brute who thought charm was reserved for those who didn't need to use their intelligence. His designer suit, an absurdly expensive thing that seemed to mock the simplicity of his heritage, couldn't hide the predatory energy that rippled beneath the surface. Candace narrowed her eyes, her fingers absently tracing the rim of her wine glass. *This is going to be unbearable.*

They had been forced to meet in neutral territory—an ancient, sprawling manor, where the vampire and werewolf factions could bicker without tearing down their own castles. But the heavy scent of tension in the air couldn't be ignored.

"You must be *Prince* Reagan," Candace drawled, her voice smooth and icy. Her sharp gaze met his with the disdain of a predator. "How lovely of you to join us."

Ronald didn't even flinch. Instead, he leaned back in his chair, his eyes twinkling with a glimmer of amusement. "Princess Sharp," he said, emphasizing the title with mockery. "I was beginning to wonder if you'd show up at all. Vampires tend to disappear when spooked, don't they?"

Candace's lips curled into a smile—one that didn't quite reach her eyes. "Unlike werewolves, who tend to appear only when it's time to make noise. How quaint." She leaned forward, her gaze locking with his. "Though, I suppose you're used to being in the spotlight. After all, you've practically made a career out of barking for the camera."

Ronald's lips parted into a grin, but his gaze hardened. "At least I have a career. It's a shame you've been reduced to a political pawn, princess. Hiding behind your family's name and a seat at the table of the dead." He took a sip of wine, his amber eyes never leaving hers. "How does it feel to be used like that?"

Candace's grip on her glass tightened, but she didn't blink. "And how does it feel to be the werewolf celebrity, always waiting for someone to throw you a bone for being a good boy with his trained tricks?"

The laughter of their respective entourages fell silent. The air in the room grew thick with the tension between the two royals, both keenly aware of the weight of the moment. This marriage—this *arranged* union—was no more than a political maneuver. A desperate attempt to bring two warring species into harmony.

Ronald's hands curled into fists beneath the table, the faint crack of his knuckles barely audible. "Careful, Princess," he said, his voice dipping into a dangerous register. "You wouldn't want me to remind you that while you *may* have royal blood, your people are just as desperate for this alliance as mine are. Don't pretend you're above it all."

The room fell into an uncomfortable silence, the weight of their words pressing down on everyone present. The waitstaff paused in their movements, and the guests exchanged uneasy glances. But neither Candace nor Ronald could look away. They were locked in a battle of pride and power, neither willing to give an inch.

"Enough," boomed her mother's voice at the end of the table, cutting through the tension like a knife. "You two will be married. There is no room for debate. It is what our elders have decided in the absence of our king!"

Candace shot a glance at her mother, her lips pressed into a thin line. Her father's absence was deeply unsettling. He had mysteriously vanished, leaving the vampires without a king, and now Candace found herself in the uncomfortable position of needing to navigate a power vacuum. It seemed she might need to find a new "daddy" to fill the role, and the thought made her stomach twist.

Ronald's jaw clenched, but he said nothing, his gaze shifting from Candace to the head of the table, where his father, the mighty Alpha of the Werewolf Kingdom, sat in grim silence.

"The wedding will take place within the month," the Alpha said firmly, his deep voice vibrating in the room as he glared at Candace. "And it will happen with or without your consent."

Candace's expression darkened. She was used to being in control of her destiny, and this marriage, this forced union, felt like an affront to everything she had worked for.

"And what of *him*?" Candace asked, her eyes narrowing as she glanced pointedly at Ronald. "Do you think your people will follow a prince who thinks more of his fame than his own family's legacy? A wolf who spends more time in the tabloids than in the council chambers?"

Ronald stood up, his chair scraping violently across the floor, but his voice remained calm, chillingly so. "A prince who stands for what he believes in. At least I'm not running away from the responsibility, unlike some people." His eyes flickered toward the empty chair at the head of the table, where her father should have been. "Where is Lord Sharp, Princess? Hiding in the shadows?"

Candace rose to her feet, her eyes blazing. "Enough. We will do as we are told. And we will make this work, if for no other reason than to avoid a war neither of our families can afford."

This marriage would happen. And for the sake of her people, her family, and the fragile peace that teetered on the edge of destruction, Candace would play her part. Even if it meant swallowing her pride—and tolerating the presence of a werewolf she couldn't stand.

The two royals would soon be bound together by blood, politics, and fate. And neither of them was ready for what came next.

6

Vows of the Night

The grand hall was cloaked in the glow of countless candles, their flames flickering against the dark stone walls. Velvet drapes in crimson and midnight blue adorned the windows, while the scent of incense curled through the air, mingling with the scent of anticipation. The cold stone beneath Candace's feet seemed to match the chill in her chest. She was draped in a gown of midnight black, the fabric as dark and flowing as the night itself.

Despite her regal poise, she couldn't quell the fluttering nerves in her stomach. Her hands were clenched at her sides, though she kept her expression serene. All eyes were on her. As the vampire princess, she had spent her life preparing for this moment, but never once had she imagined it would be like this. Forced. A political move. A calculated step toward peace between two factions that would rather see each other wiped off the face of the earth than united.

The air was thick with ancient customs and rituals tied to blood and moonlight, symbolizing the merging of two species at war. A red moon hung in the sky outside the windows, its light casting an eerie glow over the gathering.

A ceremonial chalice filled with blood stood at the altar. A token of their shared future, a bond marked by their very essence. Candace's heart skipped a beat as she glimpsed the chalice, its contents dark and tempting, much like everything that was about to unfold.

At the altar, the officiant—an elder vampire with an air of wisdom and power—spoke the sacred words. She barely listened, too focused on the figure standing beside her: Ronald Reagan, the werewolf prince. His smug arrogance was palpable, and his broad, muscular frame towered over her. His wolfish grin never seemed to leave his face as he stood there, arms crossed like this whole arrangement was little more than a personal joke.

"You're trembling, Princess," he whispered, his voice low, teasing. "What's the matter? Nervous?"

Candace turned her head sharply, her eyes narrowing. "Not at all," she snapped, though the heat in her chest betrayed her. "Perhaps it's you who should be nervous. You're about to be leashed to me, after all."

He chuckled darkly, his amber eyes gleaming. "So you enjoy playing with shackles? I'll see what I can do, Princess."

The ceremony continued with an exchange of vows—though it felt more like a performance than anything sacred. The vampire elder spoke of unity, of peace, of the importance of binding their fates together, and Ronald repeated the lines with little interest, his smirk never fading. Candace's heart raced as the final words were spoken, and a goblet of blood was presented to them. They each took a sip, the ritual binding them as husband and wife for all eternity.

* * *

The reception that followed was as awkward as it was lavish. The banquet hall was filled with dishes prepared to cater to the distinctly different diets of vampires and werewolves. The vampire side of the room was adorned with crystal goblets of blood. The werewolves, on the other hand, had whole roasted beasts on platters, the meat raw and dripping with fatty juices, the scent of it nearly overpowering.

Candace sat at the head table, her eyes flicking nervously to the werewolf side of the room where Ronald's pack feasted. She could hear their raucous laughter and the tearing of meat as they consumed it with wild abandon. The sight made her stomach turn.

"Disgusting," she muttered under her breath.

Ronald leaned in, his voice dripping with sarcasm. "What's the matter, Princess? Can't stomach a little raw meat? I thought vampires were supposed to have an iron constitution."

She shot him a venomous glare, her hand tightening around her goblet of blood. "It's vile. You people are animals."

Ronald chuckled, raising an eyebrow. "Animals, huh? I think you'll find animals quite thrilling in time."

Candace's nostrils flared as she watched him chew a chunk of meat with far too much enjoyment, his teeth glistening. "You're barbaric," she hissed, barely able to mask her revulsion.

"And you're a walking corpse," he shot back, smirking as he wiped raw juices from his lips.

Candace's hands clenched into fists at her sides, her fangs inching from her mouth. "I could tear you apart, werewolf," she growled. "Don't test me."

Ronald's grin widened, though there was a glint of challenge in his eyes. "Oh, I'd love to see you try, Princess."

The tension in the room escalated, and it was clear the guests were becoming uncomfortable with the growing animosity. It wasn't just the exchange between Candace and Ronald—the entire vampire and werewolf factions were at odds, unable to stomach one another's presence.

"Oh, I can't wait to test you. Hope you enjoy doggie style, Princess," Ronald said, his voice loud enough for the entire hall to hear.

Gasps rang through the room. The vampires recoiled in shock, their eyes flashing with anger. One particularly young vampire stood up, her eyes blazing with fury. "How dare you," she hissed.

The werewolves, for their part, looked amused. It was enough to ignite the flames of fury among the vampires, and before long, the hall erupted into chaos.

Shouting, cursing, and the sound of furniture being overturned filled the room. Candace stood from her seat, her fangs bared, ready to tear into the werewolf prince, but she was restrained by one of her elders, a firm hand placed on her shoulder.

"Enough!" the elder barked. "This is a wedding, not a battlefield!"

But it was too late. The vampires and werewolves were clashing, fangs and claws bared, sparks flying as the centuries-old hatred boiled over.

Through the chaos, Ronald's voice rang out once more, cutting through the madness. "Alright, enough. Time for us to take our leave. Let the children have their fun."

He turned toward Candace, his smirk returning, as he offered her a hand. "Shall we, Princess?"

Candace glared at him but forced herself to take his hand. Together, they left the hall, the door slamming shut behind them. Soon after, the howls coming from the bed chamber began, lasting well into the early hours of the morning.

7

Court

The weeks since the wedding had done little to calm the fire between Candace and Ronald. The vampire princess and the werewolf prince continued to clash at every turn, their marriage an endless battlefield of insults, condescension, and stubbornness. Candace had found herself sinking into old habits—being a brat, refusing to play nice, and maintaining her icy distance from the man she was bound to.

She spent most of her time locked away in their chambers or in the luxurious halls of their palace, which still felt foreign to her. Despite all the grandeur, she couldn't shake the feeling that she was trapped. But it wasn't the physical space that confined her—it was Ronald's presence, his infuriating grin, and his smug arrogance. She hated and despised him.

Candace lounged on a velvet chaise in their shared quarters one day, staring at her reflection in the ornate mirror. Her posture was elegant, of course, her perfect features framed by her dark hair. But she wasn't paying attention to her reflection. No, she was busy stewing over the very idea of being forced to attend court with Ronald. The thought of sitting beside him, playing the dutiful wife, listening to him pretend to rule—it made her want to scream.

"I'm not going," she muttered to herself, brushing a strand of hair behind her ear. "I refuse. I don't care what he says."

But moments later, there was a knock at the door, followed by Ronald's deep voice on the other side.

"Princess," he called, the mockery in his tone unmistakable, "time to get up and get moving. We're holding court in an hour."

Candace sighed dramatically, hoping he'd get the hint. But of course, he didn't. She heard the door creak open, his heavy footsteps entering the room. "Come on, don't make me drag you to the throne room like a puppy."

Candace sat up, her eyes narrowing in annoyance. "You think I'm some sort of animal you can just command?" she snapped, glaring at him.

"I think you need to learn some respect," Ronald replied, his voice dangerously calm as he took a few steps closer. His amber eyes glinted with a challenge, a dare. "Get up, or I'll leash you and drag you there myself."

Candace's eyes widened in disbelief. "You wouldn't dare."

"Oh, I absolutely would." He stepped forward, a smug grin spreading across his face as he reached for a chain that hung from his belt. "You can either walk there on your own, or I'll do it for you."

Her pride flared, and for a moment, she considered refusing outright. But something in his stance, the certainty of his words, made her bite her tongue. If she didn't go, it would only make things worse. And though she hated admitting it, the thought of him parading her like a dog was just too humiliating to entertain.

With a huff of annoyance, she stood, straightening her gown. "Fine. But don't think this means I'm going to make things easy for you."

"Wouldn't dream of it, Princess," he said, stepping aside to allow her past.

They walked through the halls in silence, the tension between them crackling like static in the air. When they entered the grand throne room, she took her seat beside Ronald. The room was already bustling with courtiers and subjects, werewolves eager to air their grievances or seek his favor. Ronald sat with an air of authority, but it was the way he conducted himself that caught Candace off guard. He wasn't the foolish, arrogant brute she had assumed he was. He was... wise.

The first subject stepped forward—a nervous werewolf with his head bowed low. "Your Highness," the man said, "the drought is killing our crops, and we are struggling. The taxes are unbearable, and we can barely feed our families."

Ronald nodded thoughtfully, his eyes never leaving the man's face. "I hear you," he said calmly, his voice carrying across the room. "It's been a hard season for many. But I've got a plan." He paused, as though allowing the weight of his words to settle in the air before continuing. "First, we'll reduce taxes on business owners. You've been burdened long enough. I'll also cut government spending where it doesn't serve us, and we'll remove the regulations that only strangle our growth. Let the businesses grow, and the money will trickle down to the people. You'll see, it'll help."

Candace listened, stunned into silence. Ronald's plan, though simplistic in its promises, was well thought out. His tone was kind, yet authoritative, and there was no trace of arrogance or bravado as he spoke. He wasn't the fool she had imagined. He wasn't just a prince of werewolves. He was a leader, someone who understood the struggles of his people and sought to make things better.

The subjects began to speak more freely, their worries addressed with a kind of understanding that Candace hadn't expected. And she couldn't help but feel a strange flicker of something—respect, perhaps? Was it possible that beneath the smug grin and the arrogance, Ronald had qualities that she admired? That he could be a good ruler?

The thought confused her, and she quickly dismissed it, unwilling to allow herself to soften toward him.

When court had finally ended, Candace slipped away from her seat and escaped toward the garden for some fresh air. The night had fallen, and the moonlight bathed the grounds in its ethereal glow. She needed space to clear her head, to think through the conflicting emotions that were threatening to surface.

But as she walked through the darkened paths, the sound of footsteps behind her caught her attention. She turned sharply, her senses alert.

Out of the shadows stepped a figure—a vampire, his posture regal and his eyes burning with fury.

"Princess Sharp," the vampire said, his voice dripping with venom. "What an abomination this marriage is. How dare you lower yourself to this… this filth?"

Candace narrowed her eyes, her fangs flickering out as she instinctively took a step back. "Who are you?"

"My name is Leonid Brezhnev," the vampire hissed. "And I've come to take you away. You don't belong here, with him. You belong with your own kind."

Before Candace could react, Leonid lunged, his grip tightening on her arm as he yanked her away from the garden path. She struggled against him, her heart racing.

"No! Let me go!" she cried, but his strength was too much.

He pulled her further into the darkness, ignoring her protests. And though she fought, she knew she wasn't strong enough to break free.

As they disappeared into the shadows, Candace couldn't help but feel a flash of fear—and something else, something deeper. A strange emptiness. She had been taken. Taken from Ronald, taken from her new life, taken from the throne she had barely settled into.

And as the night swallowed them whole, Candace realized with a sickening certainty that her life was about to take another turn.

8

The Dungeon

Candace's world was a blur of pain and confusion when she woke. Her head throbbed, her limbs heavy and sore. A damp, cold chill surrounded her, and her eyes fluttered open, only to be met by the dim glow of torchlight reflecting off stone walls.

A dungeon. She recognized the smell of dampness and old earth. Her heart raced in a panic, her breath shallow as she realized she was bound to a cold stone slab, her wrists chained above her head. The weight of the chains dragged her down, and her whole body screamed in protest, aching from hours—or perhaps days—of forced stillness. She tried to move, but the restraints held her in place.

A voice broke through the fog in her mind. "You're awake, Princess."

Candace's eyes snapped toward the figure in the shadows—a Leonid. His face was sharp, his eyes cold with disdain. He was lean, and dressed in red clothing that made him look like one of the many rebels who had opposed the union between vampires and werewolves.

"Where am I?" she spat, her voice hoarse, her throat raw from screaming.

"In a place far away from your husband," the vampire said, stepping into the light, his lips curled in a twisted smirk. "Where you'll stay until you decide to cooperate."

"Cooperate?" Candace seethed, fury bubbling up despite the fear gnawing at her insides. "Never!"

Leonid leaned closer, his eyes glinting with cold amusement. "You'll change your mind, princess. You're far more valuable than you think. Your people need you. The alliance between your kind and the werewolves is despicable. We can salvage this mess if you only give me information on the werewolf prince."

"I will never help you," Candace snarled, pulling against her chains. "You're nothing but traitors. I'd rather die than betray him!"

The vampire's smile turned cruel. "You misunderstand. I'm not asking for your cooperation. I'm giving you an ultimatum."

Candace's body tensed as she saw a wicked instrument in his hand—a garlic oil-soaked stake. "I can make this easy, or I can make it painful," he said with a quiet, chilling tone.

The next few hours passed in a blur of agony.

The vampire was relentless, torturing her with the stake, using the sharp point to press against her skin, drawing blood. He wasn't trying to kill her— no, he was trying to break her. Each cut, each burn, was designed to wear her down, to make her submit. But no matter how much pain he inflicted, Candace held firm. She refused to betray Ronald. She refused to betray the werewolves.

In her moments of delirium, the pain would ebb, and her thoughts would wander. Her mind returned to the time spent in the throne room, watching Ronald govern with such surprising skill. The way he spoke to his subjects with empathy, the way he held their respect without needing to shout or threaten. She had thought he was nothing more than a smug, arrogant celebrity, but now, she wasn't so sure.

What if... what if there was more to him than she had realized? What if he truly was a good ruler, someone who cared for his people? The thought was a knife in her heart. She had promised herself that she would never be swayed, but as she lay there, broken and exhausted, the possibility that she might have misjudged him gnawed at her.

Something stirred within her. Something deep, a yearning. Maybe—just maybe—there was some truth to what Ronald had said on their wedding night. Maybe she *did* like doggy style after all.

THE DUNGEON

The realization hit her like a punch to the gut. She was falling for him.

The sound of howling in the distance jerked Candace from her thoughts. Her heart skipped a beat, a rush of hope flooding her chest. Her mind grasped at the sound—was it... was it *him*?

Her captor, too, had heard it. His eyes narrowed, suspicious. "What's that?" he muttered under his breath, but before he could react, the door to the dungeon burst open with a loud crash.

A pack of wolves poured into the room, their eyes glowing with fury. The Leonid jumped back, snarling in surprise as the wolves advanced on him, their teeth bared.

One of the wolves stepped forward, his body massive, his fur sleek and dark, his stance commanding. His growl vibrated in the air, a low rumble of authority. "Keep your hands off my wife."

Candace's breath caught in her throat. That voice—her heart skipped a beat. There, standing before her, was none other than Ronald Reagan.

His wolf form was enormous, his muscles rippling under his dark fur, his eyes burning with an intensity that sent a shiver of both fear and desire through Candace's veins.

With one swift motion, Ronald lunged at the vampire, his claws raking through the air, knocking the rebel vampire back and into the waiting pack, literally throwing him to the wolves.

Ronald turned to her, his eyes dark and wild with emotion. Without a second thought, he shifted back into his human form, his powerful frame still rippling with strength. He stalked toward her, his gaze never leaving hers.

He reached out, unbinding the chains that held her fast. Candace barely had time to register the action before he pulled her to her feet, cradling her against him, his hands firm around her waist.

"You're mine," he growled, his lips brushing against her ear as he inhaled her scent.

Candace's breath hitched, her chest tightening with a wave of raw emotion. She felt something deep within her snap into place, something she hadn't even known was missing. He was hers. And she was his.

All the anger, all the hate she had harbored for him, melted away in that moment, leaving only desire and recognition. She had been so blind. She had fought against this fate, against him, but in truth, she had always known. Deep down, they were bound.

Ronald's hands cupped her face, his touch gentle yet urgent. "I knew it, Candace," he whispered, his voice low and rough. "From the moment I saw you, I knew you were my fated mate. I knew we would fight, we would clash, but we were meant to be together. I've always known."

Candace's chest tightened as she realized the depth of his words. The bond between them wasn't just about power, about kingdoms. It was something far older, far deeper. She hadn't been forced into this marriage. She had been chosen. It had been destiny.

"I love you," she whispered, her voice trembling.

Ronald's face softened, and for the first time since their wedding, she saw vulnerability in his eyes. He kissed her then, a kiss that spoke of all the passion, all the pain, and all the love they had both denied for far too long.

When the kiss finally broke, he pulled away slightly, his forehead resting against hers. "Let's go home," he said, his voice thick with emotion.

And with that, Ronald Reagan took her in his arms, and together, they left the dark dungeon behind. As they emerged into the moonlight, Candace finally understood that their journey, their destiny, was just beginning.

THE DUNGEON

III

Ronald + Candace

A Sonnet

9

Part I: The Meeting

Beneath the gilded halls where splendor reigns,
    Two houses met, their fates entwined by chance.
    The Reagan scion, bound by gold's domains,
    Beheld a spark within the evening's dance.

Her crimson gown, a subtle flag of war,
    Masked purpose veiled by beauty's gentle guise.
    Sweet Candace Sharp, the spy from distant shore,
    A fire of secrets burned behind her eyes.

"Your name, fair muse?" he asked with ardent tone,
    His voice a thread that wove her heart's divide.
    She smiled, though loyalty chilled her to bone—
    Could treachery and truth in love collide?

Her mission clear, her heart's resolve was steel,
    Yet in his gaze, she saw her fortress shake.
    A warmth arose she'd sworn she'd never feel,
    As fate conspired to plot her soul's mistake.

They waltzed, their steps as timeless as the stars,

RONALD AND CANDACE: A LOVE STORY

A fleeting truce beneath the chandeliers.
But shadows whispered warnings of their scars,
Of secrets buried deep, of love and fears.

For in that moment, hearts began to burn,
And yet, the world they knew could not return.

10

Part II: The Balcony

The moon ascended, casting silver light,
   Upon the garden's still and fragrant air.
   Young Ronald wandered, lost in love's delight,
   To find the balcony where she dwelt fair.

"Sweet Candace!" cried he, heart aflame with fire,
   "Though hours scarce have passed since first we met,
   Thy beauty stirs my soul, my one desire,
   Thy face, thy voice, I never shall forget!"

Above, she stood, her silhouette in shade,
   And listened, though her heart was fraught with doubt.
   A spy, she knew the price that must be paid,
   Yet love's soft whisper drowned her reason out.

"Good sir," she said, though trembling was her voice,
   "You scarcely know my name, nor I know thine."
   But still, his words made her unsure of choice,
   As love began to break her heart's design.

"I care not, dear, for house or name or creed,

RONALD AND CANDACE: A LOVE STORY

For wealth or war or all the world's affairs.
My heart is yours, if only you'll concede
To let me love you free of earthly cares!"

She faltered, for the truth she could not share,
   A daughter of the cause, sworn to deceive.
   Yet in his ardor, passion laid her bare—
   Perhaps she, too, could dare to love, believe.

The night grew still, a silent truce was born,
   Yet secrets loomed to greet the breaking morn.

11

Part III: Banishment

As dawn arose with crimson-streaked despair,
   A tide of rage swept through the house of Sharp.
   The Reagan banner flew upon the air,
   Its trumpets calling forth a battle's harp.

The clash of swords, the thunder of the fray,
   Two houses waged a war of creed and cause.
   Each stroke, a cry for victory's fleeting sway,
   Each wound, a mark of pride's unyielding laws.

Yet in the chaos, Ronald's gaze did land
   Upon his kin, their honor cast away.
   With cruel delight, one raised a savage hand
   To strike the weak and fuel the bloodied day.

"Enough!" he cried, his voice a storming flame,
   "No battle justifies this brutal sin!"
   He struck the blade from kin who bore his name,
   But as it fell, the killing blow struck in.

The world stood still—his victim met the ground,

RONALD AND CANDACE: A LOVE STORY

A brother felled by anger's blind command.
Though unintentional, the deed profound,
Left Ronald's fate to rest in justice' hand.

The Reagan lord, his visage cold and grim,
   Declared, "Your honor stained, you cannot stay.
   Though blood runs thick, you have forsaken kin—
   Henceforth, you leave our house this fateful day."

With heavy heart, he left the field of strife,
   Exiled, the weight of guilt upon his soul.
   The echoes of the war, the stolen life,
   Would haunt him as the years began to toll.

And Candace, from her hidden vantage high,
   Beheld his fall and felt her spirit break.
   For in his loss, she saw their fragile tie,
   A bond no world could mend, no heart remake.

Though battle's end brought victors' hollow pride,
   Their love remained, though torn and cast aside.

12

Part IV: A Tragic Reunion

Shadowed halls where grief and secrets lie,
   Fair Candace wove a desperate, daring scheme.
   "To flee this life, for love, I too must die,"
   She whispered soft, as hope became her dream.

A vial clenched within her trembling hand,
   Its bitter draught brought sleep's deceptive guise.
   Her breath grew still, as if by fate's command,
   And word of death spread swift through tearful cries.

When Ronald heard, his world was torn asunder,
   The stars themselves seemed cruel in heaven's dome.
   His heart, bereft, could bear no greater thunder,
   And sought to follow her to death's dark home.

With poison bought, he ventured to her side,
   To gaze upon her one last time in woe.
   Her still form lay, like beauty petrified,
   A cruel tableau where love could never grow.

"Sweet Candace, death has robbed me of my light,

RONALD AND CANDACE: A LOVE STORY

But soon, my love, we'll meet beyond the veil."
He drank the venom, sealing fate's cruel night,
And felt life's fire within him swiftly pale.

Yet in that moment, Candace stirred awake,
   Her ruse undone by love's relentless tide.
   She reached for him, her voice began to break,
   But death had claimed its prize, and would not bide.

"O dearest love!" she cried, her heart undone,
   "Why could I not foresee this fatal end?
   Without thee, life is but a hollow sun,
   A shadowed path no light can ever mend."

She found his dagger, gleaming sharp and cold,
   And pressed its edge against her heaving breast.
   "For love, I'll join thee, as the tales foretold,
   In death, our hearts will find eternal rest."

The steel did pierce, her life began to fade,
   And blood adorned the bed where love once grew.
   Two houses warred, yet here, a truce was made,
   Where death and love embraced, both fierce and true.

So fell the two, their fate forever sealed,
   A tragic bond no hatred could unweave.
   And from their loss, the world itself revealed
   A lesson love and war could not conceive.

PART IV: A TRAGIC REUNION

IV

Breaking the Ice

A Hockey Romance

13

Worlds Collide

Candace was always overwhelmed with Christmas. Sure, there was the festive music, the twinkling lights, and the warmth of family—kind of. But it was the chaos that came with her parents' blended family that she couldn't stand. The constant awkwardness, the obligatory small talk, and the too-tight spaces of her childhood home. It didn't help that her stepbrother, Shane, had decided to bring home his college roommate for Christmas break. Candace wasn't exactly thrilled by the prospect of yet another person cluttering up her personal space.

When the front door opened, Shane called out in his usual overly enthusiastic voice, "Hey, Candace! You gotta meet Ronald! He's the guy I was telling you about—the hockey player!" Candace just groaned.

"Hockey player?" She muttered under her breath as she rearranged a stack of books on the coffee table, pretending she wasn't already aware of the type.

Candace adjusted her glasses and turned to face them as Shane and the hockey player walked into the living room. He was tall. Of course, he was. And he was irritatingly handsome too—golden brown hair, broad shoulders, and that cocky smile that came with the territory of being an all-star athlete.

"Hey, I'm Ronald Reagan," he said, extending a hand. He wore a branded jacket with his team's logo, and Candace couldn't stop her eyes from narrowing at it.

"I know who you are," she replied, shaking his hand with the indifference of someone who had zero interest in hockey and even less interest in jocks.

Ronald gave her a raised brow, clearly amused by her lack of enthusiasm. "Oh, yeah? I guess you've heard about my skills on the ice. Hockey is kind of my thing. Not everyone gets the appeal, but it's a blast."

Candace tried not to roll her eyes. "Right." She flashed him a tight smile.

Shane, oblivious to the growing tension, clapped Ronald on the back. "Come on, I'm starving. Let's go see how dinner's going. Beverly making lasagna."

Ronald followed Shane into the kitchen, and Candace quickly took the opportunity to retreat to her room. She had no intention of enduring the fake politeness of dinner with Ronald, the 'golden boy.' She had enough to do on her own—like finishing the novel she'd started reading two days ago.

* * *

At dinner, the clatter of plates and glasses was interrupted by Shane's excited chatter about college life, his new classes, and Ronald's hockey exploits. Candace barely registered any of it as she pushed her food around her plate. She wasn't in the mood for small talk. She was especially not in the mood to hear about Ronald's "amazing" hockey career. It wasn't that she hated athletes—she just found them predictable and exhausting.

"So, Candace," Ronald's voice cut through the noise. "What do you like to do? You know, other than reading and stuff."

Candace's eyes narrowed, but she kept her smile fixed. "Reading and stuff? What do you mean, 'and stuff'?"

He shrugged, looking momentarily puzzled. "I don't know. People who read a lot—they're kind of… well, you know, usually they're into weird stuff."

Her face stiffened. "Weird stuff?"

"Yeah, like… who reads for fun, you know?" Ronald said, laughing at his own words.

Candace's grip tightened around her fork. She could feel the warmth rising in her cheeks, a rush of irritation flooding her system. Of all the things he could've said. He'd just insulted her most treasured pastime. She didn't let it show, though. Instead, she leaned back in her chair, smiling sweetly.

"I wouldn't expect you to understand," she said, looking pointedly at Ronald. "You know, considering how many brain cells you've probably lost from hitting a puck around and punching people."

The entire table went silent. Candace couldn't help herself—Ronald's smugness deserved a jab. She was sure he had no idea what she was talking about, but it felt good to wipe that cocky smirk off his face, even if just for a second.

Ronald's eyebrows furrowed, but he didn't rise to the bait. Instead, he quietly finished his meal, but Candace could feel his eyes occasionally flicking toward her. She ignored it, focusing on the conversation about their upcoming Christmas plans as her mom desperately tried to steer back to safer territory.

* * *

Later that night, after the house had settled into its usual post-dinner lull, Candace was in the kitchen doing the dishes. She liked to clear her head this way—just the repetitive sound of water running, the clink of dishes, and the soft hum of her music. She danced around absentmindedly, headphones on, lost in the rhythm of the song.

She didn't notice when Ronald stepped into the kitchen, leaning against the doorway until he spoke. "Hey, what're you listening to?"

Candace jumped, not expecting him to be there. She turned to face him, annoyed at how he always seemed to sneak up on her. She half-smiled, half-sneered. "It's a band you've probably never heard of. They're indie, obscure."

"Try me," Ronald said, clearly intrigued.

Candace hesitated. The last thing she wanted to do was share her music with the guy who had just insulted her favorite hobby. But then, for some reason, she found herself pulling one earbud out and holding it out to him. "Here," she muttered. "You can have this one."

Ronald raised an eyebrow before slipping the earbud into his ear. His eyes widened, a surprised smile tugging at his lips as the beat kicked in. "Okay, this is… actually kind of awesome."

Candace smirked, feeling a mix of pride and reluctance. "I told you."

He shrugged and swayed slightly to the music. "I didn't think you were the type to listen to something this… good."

Candace tilted her head. "What type do you think I am?"

Ronald looked a little sheepish, his usual cocky grin replaced by something softer. "I don't know. I guess I thought you'd be into, like, classical music or something."

"Just because I read doesn't mean I'm boring," she said, rolling her eyes, but her tone was gentler than she meant it to be.

The two of them stood there for a moment, sharing the music, the silence between them suddenly not as uncomfortable as it had been before. Candace couldn't remember the last time she felt this kind of connection with anyone.

Maybe Ronald Reagan wasn't exactly what she had expected.

But that didn't mean she was about to let him off the hook for being a hockey player.

14

Lessons in Literature

Ronald Reagan was everywhere.

Candace couldn't walk into the kitchen, the living room, or the backyard without stumbling across him. He had this infuriating ability to make himself at home, laughing with her stepdad, tossing a football with Shane, or somehow charming her mom into baking cookies. It didn't help that every time she tried to maintain her usual icy detachment, he'd flash that stupid, crooked smile and say something annoyingly likable.

And yet, she refused to let her guard down. No matter how often Ronald complimented her music taste or tried to strike up a conversation, she was determined to remain unimpressed. After all, what did she have in common with some golden boy hockey player destined for the NHL?

But then, one afternoon, everything changed.

Candace was curled up in the corner of the living room with her book when she overheard Shane and Ronald talking in the next room.

"Man, I don't know what I'm gonna do," Ronald said, his voice uncharacteristically serious. "If I fail that lit class, I'm screwed. Coach said if I don't get my grades up, I'm off the team."

"You've got time, right?" Shane replied.

"Not much. I'm barely holding on with a D. I just don't get it. Half the time

I don't even know what the professor's talking about."

Candace smirked behind her book. Typical. Of course, Ronald would struggle with literature. She was surprised he even knew how to read beyond hockey stats.

But then Shane said the words that made her blood run cold: "Candace can help you. She's great with that kind of stuff."

Candace's head snapped up. *What?*

"Really? You think she would?" Ronald asked, sounding hopeful.

"Oh, yeah," Shane said confidently. "She's a total book nerd. She'll love it."

Candace shot up from her chair and marched into the kitchen, her book still in hand. "Excuse me? I'll *love* what?"

Shane grinned at her, completely unbothered by her glare. "Ronald needs help with his literature class. You can tutor him."

"I absolutely cannot," Candace said, crossing her arms. "I don't have the time or the patience to explain *literature* to someone who thinks reading is dumb."

Ronald had the decency to look sheepish. "Okay, yeah, I deserve that. But I'm serious—I really need the help."

Candace opened her mouth to refuse again, but then she saw the look on his face. He wasn't his usual confident self. He looked... nervous. Desperate, even.

"Fine," she said with an exaggerated sigh. "I'll help you. But you owe me."

* * *

That night, Ronald knocked on her bedroom door. Candace sat cross-legged on her bed, her books spread out around her like a fortress. She gestured for him to sit on the floor.

Ronald obeyed. "Are you gonna make me write a paper about how hockey is the downfall of modern civilization?"

Candace rolled her eyes. "Depends. What book are we dealing with?"

"*The Catcher in the Rye*," he said, pulling the battered paperback out of his backpack.

Her face lit up. "I *love* this book."

Ronald looked at her skeptically. "Why? It's just some whiny kid complaining about everything."

Candace's jaw dropped. *"Whiny kid?* Ronald, Holden Caulfield is one of the most important characters in modern literature. He's a symbol of alienation and the struggle to find authenticity in a world full of phonies."

Ronald blinked at her, clearly not following.

Candace sighed and leaned forward. "Okay, think about it this way. Holden is trying to hold onto this idea of innocence—his little brother, the ducks in Central Park, and the Museum of Natural History. He doesn't want to grow up because he's afraid of becoming fake, like the adults around him. He's struggling to figure out who he is."

Something shifted in Ronald's expression as he listened. "Huh. I never thought about it like that."

"That's because you didn't think about it at all," Candace teased, but her tone was playful.

Ronald chuckled, rubbing the back of his neck. "Fair enough. But… I get it now. It's like hockey, in a way. Everyone expects me to be this perfect player, and I'm supposed to have it all figured out. But half the time, I'm just… faking it, you know?"

Candace stared at him, surprised by his honesty. "You don't seem like the type to fake anything."

He smiled faintly. "Yeah, well, I don't let it show. But it gets to me sometimes. Everyone's watching, waiting for me to screw up."

Candace nodded slowly. "I know what that's like. I mean, not the whole world watching me, but… I feel like I don't fit in here. I'm scared I'll get stuck in this town forever, like I'll never find my place."

The vulnerability in her voice made Ronald's heartache. "Hey, for what it's worth, you're pretty amazing the way you are. Smart, funny, passionate about the stuff you care about. You're not stuck, Candace. You're just waiting for the right moment to leave."

Her cheeks flushed, and she looked away, embarrassed by the way his words made her chest feel tight. "Thanks," she mumbled.

Silence fell between them, but it wasn't awkward. It was comfortable, and warm. And then, almost without thinking, Ronald reached out and brushed a strand of hair from her face, before slowly pulling away her glasses to get a better look at her eyes.

Candace froze, her breath catching as his hand lingered near her cheek. Their eyes met, and before she could stop herself, she leaned in.

The kiss was soft and hesitant, but full of unspoken emotions. When they pulled back, they both looked a little dazed.

"Well," Candace said, her voice shaky but teasing, "if that's your way of thanking me for explaining Holden Caulfield, I might have to tutor you more often."

Ronald laughed, the tension breaking, but his eyes were still locked on hers. "I wouldn't mind that."

Neither of them said it, but they both knew something had shifted between them—something they couldn't ignore.

15

Thin Ice

The ice skating rink was alive with the sounds of laughter, the scrape of blades on ice, and the hum of holiday music. Candace clung to the wall for dear life, her fingers gripping the edge as though letting go would send her plummeting into an icy abyss.

"This was a terrible idea," she muttered, her voice wavering as her skates wobbled beneath her. "I'm not meant for this. Humans weren't meant to glide across frozen water."

Ronald glided effortlessly in front of her, his movements smooth and confident. "Come on, it's not that bad," he said, grinning. "Teaching you to skate is the least I can do after you helped me understand *Catcher in the Rye*. You're the Holden Caulfield of this rink right now—clinging to safety, afraid of falling into the world."

Candace shot him a glare, but she couldn't help the small smile that tugged at her lips. "Nice try, but I'm pretty sure Holden wasn't wearing ice skates when he had his existential crisis."

Ronald laughed and extended his hand. "Okay, smartass. Let's get moving. I promise I won't let you fall."

Candace hesitated, staring at his outstretched hand. Her heart thudded in her chest, partly from fear and partly because of the way he looked at her—like he believed in her. With a deep breath, she let go of the wall and slipped her hand into his.

"See? Not so bad," he said, his voice steady and reassuring as he guided her away from the edge.

She wobbled, gripping his hand tightly, but he was there, steady and strong, keeping her upright. Slowly, with his guidance, she began to find her balance.

"Look at you!" he said, beaming. "You're skating!"

"Barely," she muttered, but there was a flicker of pride in her voice.

They circled the rink together, Ronald holding her hand the entire time. As the minutes passed, Candace began to relax, her steps becoming less hesitant. The cold air nipped at her cheeks, and the festive lights above cast a warm glow over the ice.

"This is… kind of fun," she admitted.

"Told you," he said, his grin widening. "You're a natural."

She rolled her eyes but couldn't stop smiling.

* * *

Later that evening, Candace found herself being dragged into a crowded hockey arena.

"You're seriously making me watch a hockey game?" she asked as they weaved through the crowd.

"Yup," Ronald said, his excitement palpable. "You gave *Catcher in the Rye* a chance. Now it's your turn to give hockey a shot."

"I'm pretty sure watching people beat each other up isn't the same as reading a classic novel," she quipped, but there was no real bite in her tone.

As they took their seats, the energy of the crowd washed over her. The buzz of anticipation was infectious, and despite herself, Candace felt a flicker of curiosity.

The game began, and Ronald leaned in to explain what was happening.

"Okay, so the point is to score goals by getting the puck into the other team's net," he said. "But it's not just about scoring. It's about strategy, speed, and timing."

Candace watched as the players darted across the ice, their movements fluid and precise. The crowd erupted in cheers as one player executed a perfect slap shot, sending the puck into the net.

"See that?" Ronald said, his eyes lighting up. "That's like the climax of a good book. All the buildup, the tension, and then—bam! Payoff."

Candace raised an eyebrow. "Are you seriously comparing hockey to literature?"

He grinned. "Why not? The thrill's the same. You get invested, and when everything comes together, it's magic."

As the game went on, Candace found herself drawn in. The fast pace, the near misses, the roar of the crowd—it was exhilarating. For the first time, she understood why Ronald loved it so much.

By the end of the game, she was cheering along with everyone else, her earlier skepticism forgotten.

"That was... actually amazing," she admitted as they walked back to his car.

"Told you," he said, his grin smug but endearing.

The ride back to the house was quiet at first, the post-game adrenaline still thrumming through Candace's veins. But then she turned to Ronald, her curiosity getting the better of her.

"So... what's next for you?" she asked.

He hesitated, his hands tightening on the steering wheel. "Actually... scouts from the NHL are coming to my next game. If I impress them, there's a good chance I'll get drafted."

Candace's heart sank. She should've been happy for him—this was his dream, after all. But all she could think about was how far away his dream would take him.

"That's amazing," she said, forcing a smile. "You must be excited."

"I am," he admitted, glancing at her. "But it's a lot of pressure. I've been working toward this my whole life, and it feels like everything's riding on that one game."

Candace nodded, but she couldn't shake the sinking feeling in her chest. His whole life was ahead of him, full of possibilities and opportunities. Meanwhile, she felt trapped in their small town, unsure of her own future.

When they pulled into the driveway, Candace quickly unbuckled her seatbelt. "Thanks for tonight," she said, her voice tight. "I'll see you in the morning."

Before he could respond, she was out of the car and up the stairs to her room.

Once inside, she collapsed onto her bed, the tears she'd been holding back spilling over. She hated how selfish she felt, but the truth was undeniable: Ronald Reagan was destined for bigger things, and she was terrified of being left behind.

For the first time since they'd kissed, Candace wondered if she'd made a mistake letting herself fall for him. Because no matter how much he cared about her, he would always choose hockey. And she wasn't sure her heart could handle it.

16

The Big Game

Candace stared out the window of her room, her fingers tracing the edges of the worn Russian literature book she had been reading all afternoon. She remembered how much Ronald hated Russian literature. It reminded him of America's greatest hockey rivals. But this book felt too appropriate for her mood—a novel of faith, doubt, and family, as grim and complicated as she felt inside. She could barely focus on the words; her mind kept drifting back to the ice rink, to the game that Ronald was about to play.

She couldn't bring herself to go.

The thought of seeing him out there, under all that pressure, fighting for his future while she stood helplessly on the sidelines—it was too much. She was already terrified enough of the distance between their lives, but seeing him shine in front of the scouts, surrounded by fans, would only reinforce how much she didn't belong in his world.

Her phone buzzed for the tenth time. Ronald.

She didn't want to look at it. She couldn't.

But she did.

I wish you were here. I'm trying to focus on the game, but I can't stop thinking about you. I just... I need you here, Candace. Please.

Her heart squeezed painfully in her chest. His words were so vulnerable, so unlike the confident hockey player she had known. Ronald, the golden boy of the rink, was nervous. Nervous about her.

She sighed, staring at the message. What was she supposed to do with that? She couldn't just waltz into his world and pretend everything would be fine. It was ridiculous.

The phone buzzed again. *You make me feel like I'm more than just a hockey player. I can't concentrate without you. Please come.*

Candace closed her eyes, letting the weight of his words sink in. Her resolve started to crack. She couldn't just sit here while he was out there, giving everything he had. If she meant something to him—if she was something to him—then maybe she could be there for him, just this once.

Okay, she finally typed and hit send before she could talk herself out of it. *I'm coming.*

The arena was packed when Candace arrived, the bright lights and the noise of the crowd sending her heart into overdrive. She wasn't sure where to go, and eventually took a seat in the back of the stands.

The cold air hit her face as she watched the game, her heart beating furiously. The crowd roared as the game progressed. She felt on edge, watching Ronald, her breath quick and shallow.

And then Ronald took an incredible shot, the puck sailing past the goalie and into the net. The crowd went wild, but as he skated backward to celebrate, another player—too fast, too reckless—came barreling toward him.

He didn't have time to brace himself. He was knocked hard to the ice, his body slamming against the cold surface with a sickening thud.

Candace's heart dropped to her stomach. She felt her legs give out from under her, but she kept moving, pushed by a panic she couldn't control. She wobbled onto the ice, her knees shaking, her heart racing.

She reached his side, her breath coming in sharp gasps.

Ronald lay there, his face pale, his body unmoving.

"Ronald?" she called, her voice cracking.

His eyes fluttered open, and he groaned, clearly dazed. When he saw her, his face softened, relief flooding his features.

"You... you came?" he whispered.

Candace bent down, carefully pulling him into a sitting position. "Of course, I came."

Ronald chuckled weakly. "Those ice skating lessons must've paid off, huh?"

She laughed, despite herself, brushing a lock of hair out of her face. "Shut up," she said, wiping a tear from her cheek. "You scared me."

Ronald's eyes softened. "I'll be okay. But—Candace..." He looked up at her, his voice quiet. "I don't care about the NHL. I'd give it all up for you. I'll find something else. Just... be with me."

Her heart thudded in her chest. "Ronald, that's nonsense. You've worked your whole life for this. Don't throw it away."

He shook his head, his hand reaching for hers. "No. I'd do anything. If I join the NHL, I want you there, with me. Even if it's just to sit in the stands with your book, reading. As long as you're there."

Candace's breath caught in her throat. She had never considered this possibility—Ronald, the golden boy, taking her out of the small town she feared she'd never leave. She felt torn, the weight of his offer pressing down on her chest. But deep down, she knew the truth. She couldn't ask him to sacrifice everything for her, and perhaps his offer to take her along with him was a dream come true.

"I'll go with you," she whispered, her voice thick with emotion. "I'll be there. I'll be at every game, cheering you on. Just... don't lose yourself in all of this. Promise me."

Ronald smiled, his eyes sparkling with gratitude and something else—a promise. "I promise."

The next morning, the newspaper showed a photo on the front page of the sports section—Ronald and Candace, kissing on the ice. The photo appeared alongside the headline that would change Ronald's life: *Reagan Makes the Cut: NHL Scouts Choose the Star Forward for the Pros.*

But the picture wasn't just about the game. It was about the promise they had made to each other, to navigate the unknown hand in hand, even when the world seemed to pull them in different directions.

And as Candace looked at Ronald Reagan, her hand in his, she knew that no matter where life took them, they would find their way—together.

RONALD AND CANDACE: A LOVE STORY

V

Power and Passion

A Mafia Romance

17

The Snare

The night was cold, and the fog clung to the alleyway like a second skin. A silver car idled at the end of the narrow street, its engine purring softly, a stark contrast to the danger that lingered in the air. Inside the car, Ronald Reagan, mob boss of The Eagles, leaned back in the passenger seat, eyes narrowed as he scanned the shadows. His right-hand man, George Bush, sat beside him, his fingers drumming impatiently against the leather of the seat.

"She'll come this way," Ronald said, his voice low and confident. "She always does."

Bush glanced at him, his brow furrowing in the dim light. "You sure about this, boss? Her father's not someone to piss off lightly. And her... she's not exactly someone to underestimate."

Ronald's lips twitched in a half-smile. "I'm not underestimating her, George. I'm counting on her."

Candace Sharp was the daughter of a feared mafia boss, the ruthless leader of the Hammer and Sickles. The rumors about her were as dark as they came—beautiful, cold, and with a fire that matched her father's. But Ronald Reagan didn't fear her. He respected her as a tool, nothing more. Her father owed him, and she was going to be the leverage he needed to collect.

A soft sound broke the silence—footsteps. They echoed against the concrete walls, growing closer, sharper. Ronald's eyes flicked to the corner of the alley, and there she was.

Candace Sharp, her silhouette shaped against the fog, walked with the grace of someone who was used to power, used to fear. She was alone, as always. A briefcase hung loosely in her hand, her heels clicking with purpose. Her brown hair glowed under the streetlights, a halo of gold that only highlighted the cold steel of her expression.

"This is it," Ronald murmured, his voice turning hard.

The two men stepped out of the shadows, surrounding her in a quick, practiced movement. Candace didn't flinch. Her eyes flicked from one man to the other, calculating, unafraid.

"Well, well, Candace Sharp," Ronald said smoothly, taking a step closer. "You're exactly where we want you."

Candace's lips curled into a thin, contemptuous smile. "I knew this was coming," she said, her voice steady, unshaken. "You think you can use me against my father?"

"We don't think," Ronald replied, his voice carrying a hint of menace now. "We know. He owes us. And we're using you to make sure he pays up."

Her smile faded slightly, but she didn't back down. "You won't break him with me. He'll never give in. You're wasting your time."

"We'll see about that." Ronald nodded to Bush, who stepped forward, grabbing her by the arm with the kind of force that told her he wasn't asking for compliance. "Get in the car, Candace."

Candace resisted, her eyes flashing with fury, but she knew the moment she fought back, it would only get worse. Slowly, she allowed herself to be guided toward the car. The door slammed shut behind her, sealing her fate.

* * *

The mansion loomed ahead, a grand, imposing structure bathed in the soft light of the street lamps. It was a different world, one Candace hadn't ever imagined she'd be a part of. She had always been surrounded by the raw, gritty reality of her father's operations, but here—here was something almost unnatural, something more sinister.

She was escorted through the grand halls, her footsteps echoing against the polished marble floors, as Ronald and George led her to a room that could have been plucked from a dream. The walls were draped in rich tapestries, the furniture sleek and modern, yet comfortable. A large bed covered in fine linen dominated the room, with large windows offering a view of the city below. Everything was designed for luxury, a luxury she hadn't expected from the men who had just dragged her into their clutches.

"Make yourself comfortable," Ronald said, though his tone was far from polite. "You'll be staying here for a while. We'll check in later."

Candace's gaze flicked to him, her eyes cold. "You really think this is going to work, don't you?"

Ronald's smile never faltered. "I don't need to think. I already know."

And with that, they left her alone, the heavy door clicking shut behind them. Candace stood in the center of the room, her chest tight, the silence closing in around her. She was alone. Truly alone. The tears she had been holding back for so long finally started to fall, hot and relentless.

Candace Sharp, daughter of a mob kingpin, a woman who had never shown weakness, collapsed onto the bed, her sobs echoing through the room. The walls didn't comfort her. The luxury didn't matter. She had been trapped, and there was no way out.

Not yet. But there would be.

She would find a way.

18

Cracks in the Mask

The days blurred together, marked only by the passage of sunlight streaming through the tall windows of the room. Candace lay on the bed, motionless, her back to the door. The untouched trays of food were taken away and replaced with fresh ones, but she paid them no mind. Sleep came and went in restless snatches, but when she was awake, her thoughts were a haze of anger, fear, and something darker—hopelessness.

Ronald Reagan stood in the doorway, arms crossed, his cold blue eyes fixed on her motionless figure. His jaw clenched as he noted the untouched meal on the nightstand. It had been days now, and she hadn't eaten a thing. At first, he had shrugged it off. Let her starve herself if she wanted; it would make her easier to handle. But as the hours ticked by, unease crept in.

"Boss, this isn't good," George Bush had told him earlier, his tone unusually grim. "She's gonna get sick if she keeps this up. That's not what we need right now."

Reagan had waved him off, but George's words had stuck. And now, standing here, watching the faint rise and fall of Candace's shoulders, he felt something twist in his chest—an unfamiliar pang he wasn't sure he liked.

"Candace." His voice was sharp, commanding.

She didn't stir.

He stepped closer, his footsteps echoing on the hardwood floor. "You can't keep this up," he said, his tone softening despite himself. "You're not doing yourself any favors."

Still no response.

Ronald sighed, raking a hand through his dark hair. He pulled the chair from the desk and sat down beside the bed. "Look, you're stubborn. I get it. But starving yourself isn't going to solve anything. If you want to fight back, you need your strength."

Her shoulders tensed, just barely, but it was enough to tell him she was listening.

"I'll make you a deal," he said, leaning forward, his elbows resting on his knees. "You eat something—anything—and I'll leave you alone for the rest of the day. Hell, you don't even have to say thank you."

There was a long silence before she finally turned her head to look at him, her eyes red and puffy, her face pale. "You really think you're going to win me over with a sandwich?" she croaked, her voice hoarse from disuse.

Ronald allowed a small smile to tug at the corner of his mouth. "I'd settle for a bite of toast."

* * *

The next morning, Candace surprised him. She emerged from her room, her steps tentative as she made her way down the grand staircase. Ronald and George were seated at the long dining table in the sunlit kitchen, their conversation halting the moment they noticed her.

"Well, look who decided to join us," George said, his grin breaking the tension.

Candace didn't respond, but her eyes darted around the room, taking in her surroundings. The kitchen was warm and inviting, a surprising contrast to the cold, calculating men who ran the house.

"Sit," Ronald said, gesturing to the chair across from him.

She hesitated but eventually complied, her stomach growling audibly as the aroma of freshly cooked food filled the air. George piled a plate high with eggs, bacon, and toast, sliding it across the table to her.

"Eat up," he said. "You'll need your strength."

She took a tentative bite, the flavors exploding on her tongue after days of nothing. The men watched her closely, but for once, it didn't feel threatening.

As the meal progressed, Candace began to speak, her voice stronger now. "You're wasting your time, you know."

Ronald raised an eyebrow. "And why's that?"

She hesitated, then put her fork down, meeting his gaze directly. "Because I don't know where my father is. No one does. He... disappeared months ago. Even I don't know how to reach him."

The room fell silent. Ronald leaned back in his chair, his expression unreadable, while George exchanged a worried glance with him.

"You're lying," Ronald said, though his tone lacked conviction.

"I'm not," Candace insisted, her voice steady. "If I knew where he was, I wouldn't have been walking down that alley alone. I wouldn't have been in this position."

Ronald studied her for a long moment before nodding slowly. "If that's true... it complicates things."

She leaned forward, her voice lowering. "So what now? Do you kill me because I'm useless to you?"

His gaze hardened, but there was no malice in it. "No. I'm not going to hurt you, Candace. Not now, not ever. Whatever happens, you'll be safe here."

She blinked, caught off guard by the sincerity in his voice. For the first time, she saw a glimpse of the man beneath the cold exterior—a man who, despite everything, didn't want to see her hurt.

Back in her room, Candace sat on the edge of the bed, her mind racing. She had expected him to lash out, to threaten her, but instead, he had promised her safety. It didn't make sense.

Meanwhile, Ronald remained in the kitchen, his coffee growing cold in front of him. George stood at the counter, watching him carefully.

"She's telling the truth," George said finally.

Ronald didn't respond, his mind too tangled to focus. If Candace didn't know where her father was, their plan was useless. But it wasn't just the failure of the plan that bothered him—it was her. The image of her breaking down in that room, the raw pain in her voice, stayed with him.

For the first time in years, Ronald Reagan didn't know what to do.

19

Alliances and Affection

Candace wandered through the sprawling mansion, her fingers trailing along the smooth walls as she explored the labyrinth of rooms and hallways. It had been a week since her arrival, and she was beginning to acclimate to the rhythm of life under Ronald Reagan's roof. Still, there was a sense of unease, a lingering tension that never quite left her.

Her curiosity got the better of her as she pushed open a heavy wooden door at the end of a quiet hallway. The room she stepped into was unlike anything else in the house. It was spacious, with cream-colored walls curving gently to form a peculiar oval shape. A large, imposing desk sat in the center, flanked by leather chairs and shelves lined with books and documents.

Ronald Reagan sat behind the desk, his dark suit tailored to perfection, exuding authority. Around him were a handful of men, all of them leaning forward in their seats, their faces grim. George Bush stood by the window, arms crossed, nodding as someone spoke.

Candace froze, realizing she had walked into what was clearly an important meeting. But instead of scolding her, Reagan's gaze flicked to her for a brief moment, his expression unreadable. He didn't tell her to leave, so she stayed, lingering by the doorway as she listened.

"Sharp's men are moving in fast," one of the men said, his voice clipped. "We've already lost two key locations in the East District this week. If we don't act soon, we'll lose control completely."

"Hammer and Sickles have the manpower and the cash flow," another added. "They're choking us out, and we don't have the resources to hold them off forever."

Reagan's face remained stoic, but there was a flicker of frustration in his eyes. "We need a strategy. Something decisive. I won't let the Hammer and Sickles take what's ours."

Candace stepped forward before she could stop herself. "You're going about this all wrong," she said, her voice clear and steady.

The room fell silent, every head turning toward her. Reagan leaned back in his chair, one eyebrow raised in surprise. "Do enlighten us, Miss Sharp."

She crossed her arms, her confidence growing as she spoke. "My father's men don't attack blindly. If they're targeting your East District, it's because he's identified a weakness. Likely a distribution route or a key asset. He's not just trying to take territory—he's trying to cripple your operations."

The men exchanged uncertain glances, but Reagan kept his eyes on her, intrigued. "And you know this how?"

"Because I've seen them do it before," she replied, shrugging. "You need to focus on securing your supply chains. Strengthen your defenses where he expects you to be weak. And then…" She hesitated, a sly smile playing on her lips. "Hit him where it hurts. He's got a shipment coming in tomorrow night at the docks. Take that, and you'll force him to back off—at least for now."

Reagan tilted his head, considering her words. "You're awfully forthcoming with information about your own family."

She met his gaze without flinching. "My father left me to fend for myself. I don't owe him anything."

A slow smile spread across Reagan's face. He turned to his men. "You heard her. Tighten security on our routes and prep a team for the docks tomorrow night. George, I want this handled smoothly."

George nodded, already making notes.

The meeting adjourned, and the men filtered out, leaving Candace and Reagan alone in the oval-shaped office. He stood, his imposing figure casting a long shadow across the room.

"You've got guts," he said, walking toward her. "And a sharp mind. I'm impressed."

Candace arched a brow. "What can I say? I like proving people wrong."

His lips twitched into a rare smile. "Come on. Let's get out of here."

She blinked, caught off guard. "What?"

"I'm taking you out," he said, his tone leaving no room for argument. "You've earned it."

* * *

The shopping spree was unlike anything Candace had ever experienced. Reagan escorted her through high-end boutiques, insisting she try on dresses, shoes, and jewelry that made her blush with their price tags. Every time she hesitated, he waved her off, his charm disarming her protests.

"You're my princess to spoil," he said with a grin, handing the clerk his black card.

The words sent a strange warmth through her chest, though she brushed it off, refusing to let herself get caught up in the moment.

They ended the evening at a lavish restaurant, where the waitstaff treated them like royalty. Over a candlelit dinner, Reagan asked her questions—about her childhood, her likes and dislikes. She found herself opening up more than she expected, her guard slipping as he listened intently, his cold exterior softening with each passing moment.

For the first time in years, Candace felt... seen.

When they returned to the mansion, Candace's arms were laden with shopping bags, and her heart was unexpectedly light. At the top of the staircase, Reagan stopped her, his expression unreadable.

"You did good today," he said quietly.

She smiled, unsure how to respond. "Thanks... for everything."

Without a word, he leaned down and pressed a kiss to her forehead, lingering just long enough for her to feel the heat of it. Her breath hitched, her cheeks warming as he pulled away.

"Goodnight, Candace," he said, his voice softer than she'd ever heard it.

"Goodnight," she whispered, watching as he walked down the hallway and disappeared into the shadows.

Candace retreated to her room, her mind racing. The kiss had been brief, chaste, but it had ignited something inside her she hadn't felt before—a spark of hope, a flicker of trust.

And maybe, just maybe, something more.

20

The Sickle and The Eagle

Ronald Reagan sat at the head of the table in his office, his phone pressed to his ear, his expression dark. Candace lingered in the doorway, watching the way his jaw tightened as the person on the other end spoke. She couldn't hear the words, but she didn't need to—she could tell from his reaction that it was about her.

When he hung up, he turned to her, his eyes locking onto hers with an intensity that sent a chill down her spine.

"That was the Hammer and Sickles," he said, his voice low. "They want to negotiate for you."

Candace felt her heart skip a beat. She should have been relieved—this was her chance to go back, to leave behind the gilded cage Ronald had built for her. But instead of relief, all she felt was a hollow ache in her chest. She didn't want to go back.

"They're willing to trade," he continued. "But I'm not convinced it's a trade worth making."

"Ronald…" Her voice faltered as she stepped closer. "What are you going to do?"

He looked at her, his gaze softening in a way that made her feel both exposed and safe. "What I always do, princess. Protect what's mine."

* * *

The meeting was set for the following evening at an abandoned warehouse on the outskirts of the city—a neutral location chosen to prevent any side from having the upper hand. Reagan's men arrived first, taking strategic positions around the perimeter. Candace stayed close to Ronald, her fingers curling into the fabric of his coat as they waited.

The Hammer and Sickles arrived in force, their black SUVs rolling up like sharks cutting through still water. A tall man with a scar running down his cheek stepped out, flanked by armed guards. Candace recognized him as her father's replacement, Dmitry.

"Ronald Reagan," Dmitry said, his voice echoing in the cavernous space. "We're here for the girl."

Ronald stood his ground, his hand resting lightly on Candace's lower back. "You're not getting her," he said simply.

Dmitry's eyes narrowed. "She's not yours to keep."

"She's not yours to take back," Reagan shot back, his tone sharp as a blade. "Your boss abandoned her. Left her in the cold while he ran off to save his own skin. And now you want her back? Not a chance. She's with me now. She's mine." He glanced down at her, his expression softening. "I'm her daddy now."

Candace's heart twisted at his words. She should have been furious, humiliated even, but all she felt was a strange, undeniable warmth.

Dmitry's face darkened. "Then I guess we'll take her by force."

The first gunshot shattered the tense silence, and chaos erupted.

Reagan's men moved quickly, their training evident as they returned fire and shielded Candace from harm. She crouched behind a stack of crates, her heart pounding in her chest as bullets whizzed past. Reagan stayed close, his gun in hand, his movements precise and calculated.

"Stay down!" he barked, his voice cutting through the cacophony.

She nodded, her eyes wide as she watched him take out one of Dmitry's men with a single, well-placed shot. But then she saw it—out of the corner of her eye, a flash of movement.

"Ronald, look out!" she screamed.

He turned just as the bullet hit him, tearing through his left armpit. He staggered, his gun clattering to the ground as he collapsed.

"No!" Candace scrambled to his side, her hands shaking as she pressed them against the wound, trying to stem the bleeding. "Ronald, stay with me!"

George appeared, his face grim as he knelt beside them. "It's bad, but he'll live," he said, ripping a strip of fabric from his shirt to make a temporary bandage. "We just need to get him to the hospital."

Reagan groaned, his face pale but determined. "Not… yet," he said, his voice weak. He grabbed George's arm, forcing him to stop. Then his eyes found Candace, his gaze burning despite the pain.

"Candace," he rasped. "I don't care what happens tonight… I need you to know something."

She leaned closer, tears streaming down her face. "What is it?"

"I love you," he said, his voice cracking. "I want you to stay with me… forever. Be the princess of my empire. Marry me."

Her breath hitched, her heart pounding in her chest. In that moment, surrounded by chaos, she realized there was only one answer.

"Yes," she whispered, her voice breaking. "I'll marry you."

The remaining men managed to drag Reagan to safety, Dmitry and the Hammer and Sickles retreating when they realized they were outmatched. Reagan was rushed to the hospital, where the doctors patched him up and assured Candace he would make a full recovery.

Weeks later, Reagan stood at the altar in a private ceremony held in the mansion's grand hall, his arm still in a sling but his smile brighter than she'd ever seen it. Candace walked toward him in a flowing white dress, her heart full as she realized she was exactly where she was meant to be.

The vows they exchanged were simple but heartfelt, their love forged in the fire of danger and devotion.

And as Ronald Reagan leaned down to kiss his bride, his empire celebrated the coronation of its new princess.

THE SICKLE AND THE EAGLE

VI

Love Across The Eras

A Time-Travel Romance

21

A Brush With Time

Candace Sharp adjusted the strap of her leather tote bag as she stepped onto Pennsylvania Avenue, the cool fall air brushing against her cheeks. The city buzzed with history, and she couldn't help but feel a twinge of awe at the sight of the White House looming in the distance.

Her mother's voice echoed in her mind: *D.C. is the perfect place to figure out your next move, Candace. You need inspiration.* Inspiration, she thought wryly, wasn't the issue. She just didn't know what she was looking for.

The tour of the White House was her last stop before heading back to her hotel. As she walked through the grand halls, her sneakers squeaking against the polished floors, she listened half-heartedly to the tour guide's speech about American presidents. She had always loved history, but today, her mind was adrift.

Until she saw the painting.

It hung in a quiet corner, away from the main displays, as if forgotten by time. The man in the portrait had an undeniable presence. His strong jawline, intense gaze, and slight, knowing smile made her stop mid-step. Candace drew closer, unable to resist the pull of his piercing blue eyes. The plaque beneath the painting simply read: *Ronald Reagan.*

"Wow," she murmured, tilting her head. She didn't remember Reagan looking *this* striking in her history books. It was as though the artist had captured not just his likeness but a magnetic energy that seemed to reach out to her. She glanced around to make sure no one was watching, then tentatively extended her fingers toward the canvas.

The instant her fingertips grazed the surface, the world spun violently. A rush of wind roared in her ears, and the room dissolved into a kaleidoscope of colors. Candace barely had time to gasp before her feet hit solid ground.

She stumbled, catching herself against the smooth surface of a desk. The air was different here—warmer, and scented faintly with cigar smoke and leather. She blinked, her heart racing as she took in her surroundings. Heavy drapes framed the windows, sunlight spilling onto a desk stacked with papers. A pair of men in dark suits stood nearby, their sharp eyes narrowing as they noticed her.

"Who the hell are you?" one of them barked, reaching for his earpiece.

"I…" Candace stammered, realizing she was in an office that looked suspiciously like the Oval Office. *This can't be real.*

The other man stepped forward, his hand hovering near the gun on his belt. "How did you get in here?"

"I… I don't know," she managed, her voice trembling. "There was a painting, and I touched it, and…"

"Stand down," a calm voice cut through the tension. The men turned as a figure entered the room, his presence commanding yet oddly reassuring.

Candace's breath hitched. It was *him* — the man from the painting. Ronald Reagan, in the flesh.

"Mr. President," one of the agents said, stepping aside. "We don't know who she is or how she got here."

Reagan's eyes flicked to Candace, his expression softening as he took in her wide-eyed confusion. "At ease, gentlemen," he said. "I'm sure there's an explanation."

Candace opened her mouth, but no words came out. How could she possibly explain this?

"She's my new intern," Reagan said smoothly, offering her a faint smile. "Must be her first day. Isn't that right, Miss…?"

"Sharp," she blurted. "Candace Sharp."

The Secret Service agents exchanged skeptical glances but stepped back at

Reagan's nod. "I'll take it from here," he said.

When they were alone, Reagan gestured toward a chair. "Have a seat, Miss Sharp."

Candace sank into it, her hands gripping the armrests as if the world might spin out from under her again. Reagan sat across from her, studying her with a mix of curiosity and concern.

"Now," he said, his tone gentle. "Why don't you tell me who you really are?"

Candace took a deep breath. "You're going to think I'm crazy," she said.

"Try me," he replied, leaning back.

"I… I'm not from here. Not from this time, I mean." She hesitated, then plunged ahead. "I'm from the future. 2024."

Reagan's brow furrowed, but he didn't interrupt. "I was on a tour of the White House, and I saw your painting. When I touched it, I ended up here. I don't know how or why, but…" She gestured helplessly. "Here I am."

Silence stretched between them as Reagan considered her words. Finally, he leaned forward, resting his elbows on his knees. "That's quite a story," he said carefully.

"It's the truth," Candace insisted, her voice rising. "I don't know how to prove it, but…"

He held up a hand, his expression calm. "Let's say I believe you," he said. "Until we figure this out, you'll need to keep a low profile. Time travel, if that's what this is, isn't something the world is ready to hear about."

Candace nodded, relief flooding through her. "Thank you," she said softly.

Reagan's smile returned, faint but reassuring. "Don't mention it," he said. "For now, Miss Sharp, consider yourself part of my staff. We'll find a way to get you home."

As she followed him out of the office, Candace couldn't help but feel a strange sense of safety in his presence. But beneath it all, a question gnawed at her: *What if I can never go back?*

22

Out of Place

Candace Sharp stared at the stack of documents on her borrowed desk in the West Wing. Words blurred together as she tried to make sense of the reports and memos, all written in a style that felt foreign to her. Every time she thought she understood the task, another question cropped up: How did these people function without email? Or messenger? The analog chaos of the 1980s was charming in theory, but in practice, it was a maze of typewriters, filing cabinets, and handwritten notes.

Her fellow staffers didn't make it any easier. They'd been polite, but there was an air of skepticism about her sudden appearance. "Reagan's new intern," they called her, though their eyes said, *Who is she really?*

Candace sighed and flipped through another set of memos, trying to ignore the tight knot in her chest. She felt out of place, like a puzzle piece forced into the wrong box. But what choice did she have? Until she and President Reagan figured out how to send her back to her own time, she had to survive here.

That evening, as the halls of the White House grew quieter, Candace found herself alone in the Oval Office. The room glowed with warm light from the desk lamp, and the scent of polished wood and leather filled the air. She was sorting through yet another stack of documents when the door creaked open.

"Still working, Miss Sharp?"

She looked up to see Ronald Reagan standing in the doorway, his signature smile softening the lines of his face. He stepped inside, the door clicking shut behind him. He was dressed in a tailored suit, his tie slightly loosened as though he'd just finished a long day.

"I didn't realize the time," she admitted, pushing a stray lock of hair behind her ear. "There's... a lot to do."

He chuckled, walking toward her. "There always is. But you've been doing a fantastic job."

Candace blinked. "Really? Because most days, I feel like I'm drowning."

Reagan rested a hand on the edge of the Resolute Desk and leaned slightly forward. "It's a learning curve. No one expects you to know everything right away."

"Thanks," she said, her voice soft. "It's just... weird. I've never felt like I fit in anywhere. Not back home, and definitely not here." She hesitated, then added, "But sometimes, I think I'm supposed to be here. Like I... belong, somehow."

Reagan's gaze grew thoughtful. "Perhaps there's something to that," he said. "Fate has a funny way of putting people where they're needed most, even if it doesn't make sense at first."

Her heart skipped a beat at the sincerity in his voice. There was a warmth in his expression, a genuine kindness that made her feel seen in a way she hadn't felt in years.

"Maybe," she said, her lips curving into a shy smile. "I guess I'll have to see how it plays out."

For a moment, they stood in comfortable silence, the hum of the desk lamp the only sound in the room. Candace's cheeks warmed as she realized how close they were standing, his steady gaze lingering on her as if he, too, was trying to decipher what her presence here meant.

She cleared her throat, breaking the spell. "I should probably get going. Long day tomorrow, right?"

Reagan straightened, his smile returning. "Of course. Rest well, Miss Sharp."

"Goodnight, Mr. President," she said, gathering her things. As she slipped past him toward the door, she caught one last glance at his thoughtful expression and felt the faint pull of something unspoken between them.

As she walked back to her quarters, her heart was still fluttering. Perhaps the 1980s weren't where she belonged—but maybe, just maybe, there was a reason she was here. And it had everything to do with Ronald Reagan.

23

A Night To Remember

Weeks passed, and Candace began to find her rhythm in the bustling world of the White House. Thanks to Ronald's patient guidance, she learned to navigate the labyrinth of government work. His words of encouragement buoyed her on tough days, and she started to feel like she was truly contributing.

One evening, Reagan approached her desk with an unusual request.

"Miss Sharp," he began, a playful glint in his eye, "I'd like you to accompany me to a ball tomorrow evening."

Candace's eyebrows shot up. "Me? At a ball?"

He smiled. "You have a good eye, and I could use someone I trust. These events aren't just for show—we're always watching for potential threats, especially from the Russians. Think of it as part of your duties."

"I... I'd be honored," she stammered, unsure whether to feel flattered or terrified.

The next evening, a stunning blue gown was delivered to her quarters. Its shimmering fabric and elegant cut made her feel like royalty. When she arrived at the ballroom, her heart fluttered as Reagan turned to greet her. His gaze swept over her, lingering for a beat too long.

"You look breathtaking," he said softly, his voice carrying an unspoken weight. He offered his arm, and she took it, her pulse quickening at the warmth of his touch.

Throughout the evening, Reagan's hand remained at the small of her back, a steady presence that sent shivers up her spine. His fingers brushed lightly against her as he guided her through the crowd, leaning close to whisper names, anecdotes, and subtle warnings about the guests.

"See that man by the buffet?" he murmured, his breath warm against her ear. "He's one to watch. Quick to charm, but he has a knack for twisting words."

Candace nodded, her skin tingling where his lips had come dangerously close. She couldn't focus on the man by the buffet—her thoughts were consumed by the man at her side. The way his hand never strayed, the way his voice softened when he spoke to her—it was intoxicating.

"You're doing wonderfully," he whispered later, as they paused near the edge of the room. "I knew I could count on you."

Her cheeks flushed. "I'm just following your lead."

He chuckled, his eyes crinkling at the corners. "You're modest, Miss Sharp. But you've been indispensable tonight."

As the ball wound down, Candace felt a mixture of relief and longing. She'd spent the evening acutely aware of Reagan's every movement, every glance, and now, as they made their way back to the White House, the tension between them felt nearly unbearable.

Back in the Oval Office, Reagan loosened his tie and sank into his chair, the weight of the evening settling on his shoulders.

"You were incredible tonight," he said, motioning for her to sit across from him. "I couldn't have done it without you."

Candace smiled, though she could see the exhaustion in his eyes. "You're giving me too much credit. You're the one carrying the weight of the world."

He exhaled deeply, his gaze dropping to the desk. "Sometimes, I wonder if I'm doing the right thing. Every decision feels like it could change everything—for better or worse. It's overwhelming."

Candace leaned forward, her voice steady and sincere. "You're doing an incredible job. I've seen firsthand how much you care about this country. You inspire people, Mr. President. Don't ever doubt that."

Reagan looked up, his eyes meeting hers. "Thank you, Candace. That means more than you know."

The air between them shifted, charged with something unspoken. Slowly, he rose from his chair and walked around the desk, stopping just in front of her. She stood instinctively, her breath hitching as he reached for her hand.

"Maybe…" he began, his voice low, "maybe I'm the reason you came here. To this time. To me."

Her heart pounded as he leaned in, his lips brushing against hers in a kiss that was as tender as it was electrifying. Time seemed to stop, the only sound was the soft rustle of fabric as she moved closer to him.

When they finally pulled apart, Reagan's expression was a mix of resolve and longing. Without a word, he walked to the door and turned the lock, the click echoing in the quiet room.

"Candace," he said, his voice thick with emotion, "I don't know what tomorrow will bring, but tonight, I'm sure of one thing."

She swallowed hard, her gaze never leaving his. "What's that?"

"You're mine."

In that moment, the weight of their connection became undeniable, a force neither could resist. The night stretched on, filled with whispered confessions and a passion neither could ignore.

24

I Will Find You

Candace stepped into the White House the next morning, the familiar marble floors cold beneath her feet, but something was different. The usual hum of activity, and the quiet efficiency of the staff, felt off. There was a hushed undertone to every conversation, a whispering tension that gripped the air. As she made her way to her desk, she couldn't help but notice the way people glanced at her—quick, furtive glances followed by hurried whispers that died down as soon as she approached. It was like the entire building was holding its breath, waiting for something to break.

At first, Candace thought it was just the usual office gossip. But the more she tried to focus on her work, the clearer it became. They were talking about her. The weight of their stares felt too heavy, the sudden silence when she walked into a room too obvious.

She couldn't bear the curiosity gnawing at her anymore. She had to find him.

She left her desk in a flurry of motion, her heart beating faster as she approached the Oval Office. The door was slightly ajar, and she knocked gently, pushing it open with a sense of urgency.

What she saw inside made her stop dead in her tracks. Ronald stood at his desk, his face pale, his normally commanding posture slouched. His suit was rumpled, his tie crooked, and he looked nothing like the confident, unwavering man who had led the country so fearlessly. The bags under his eyes were darker than she'd ever seen.

His advisors, standing off to the side, exchanged glances filled with disdain. One of them, a tall man with harsh features, shot Candace a look that could have cut glass. But before he could say a word, Ronald's voice rang out sharply, breaking the tension.

"Leave us," he commanded, his tone laced with an edge that startled Candace. The advisors hesitated, looking from Ronald to Candace, but when Ronald's glare hardened, they silently filed out of the room.

Once they were alone, Candace rushed forward, concern flooding her chest. "Ronald, what's going on? What's happened?"

He sighed deeply, running a hand through his hair, his exhaustion evident. "I should have known this would catch up with us." His voice was low, almost broken. He met her gaze, his eyes filled with regret. "There have been spies, Candace. Tapping the Oval Office. They know about us. Everything we've shared… it's out there now."

Candace's heart sank, remembering the things they had shared in the Oval Office after the ball. It would be a matter of time until they discovered the stain on her blue dress. She felt a cold shiver run down her spine. "What do you mean? Are we… are we in danger?"

He nodded grimly. "Yes. Your involvement with me… with my administration… it could ruin everything. Not just for me, but for you too. The people will turn against you, Candace. They'll use it all—our relationship, everything—to tear me down, and destroy you in the process."

Candace shook her head, disbelief flooding her chest. "But we didn't do anything wrong. You're the president. You can—"

He cut her off, his voice thick with emotion. "I *can't*, Candace. I can't drag you down with me. I love you too much to let that happen. You deserve more than to be tangled in all this… politics. It's dangerous, and it's never going to stop."

A silence hung in the air between them, and Candace's mind raced. She had to do something. She had to protect him, protect them both.

"Maybe… maybe if I go back to my time," Candace said, her voice tentative, "the world will forget about me. Forget I was ever involved in your life."

Ronald's expression twisted in agony. "I can't let you go, Candace. I—"

"You have to," she interrupted gently, stepping closer to him. "You have to for both of us. For America. If I disappear, no one will remember that I was ever here. No one will know. It'll be like nothing ever happened, and you can continue being the strong leader this country needs."

He closed his eyes, his jaw tightening, fighting with himself. "I can't lose you, Candace. You're everything to me."

But Candace's resolve was firm. "You'll still have everything. You'll still have your presidency. And I... I will find a way back. Somehow. Maybe one day, I'll come back to you."

She took a step back, her heart aching at the thought of leaving him. "But I need to go. For you. For us."

Ronald stared at her, his lips parted as if searching for words, but none came. Finally, he gave a slow nod, the weight of his decision crushing him. "If that's what you think is best..."

Candace moved to the portrait of him, the one that had first brought her here. The dark, brooding image of the man who had captured her heart. She reached out, her fingers trembling as they hovered over the painted surface.

Ronald stood behind her, his presence a comforting yet painful warmth. "Goodbye, Candace," he whispered.

She turned to face him, her eyes brimming with tears. "Goodbye, Ronald. I'll always remember you."

"Candace," he said, his voice strained. "No matter where you go, I will find you. Through time, through space, no matter what, I will always find you. I swear it."

She smiled through her tears, her heart breaking but filled with love. "I know you will."

With one last, lingering glance, Candace touched the painting, her fingers pressing against the cool canvas. The room around her seemed to fade, the world shifting as she was pulled away from everything she knew.

In the blink of an eye, Candace found herself back in 2024.

She stood alone in her apartment, her hands still trembling from the encounter. The quiet hum of the modern world felt foreign to her now.

But as her mind settled, the image of Ronald lingered, a haunting presence in her thoughts. She knew, deep in her bones, that no matter where she went, Ronald Reagan would haunt her for the rest of her life. And that was enough for her.

   He would always be with her, across time and space.

Made in the USA
Columbia, SC
19 December 2024